The Dragon in the Christmas Tree

Merry Christmas Mason!!

BY PATRICK W. LEDRAY

ILLUSTRATED BY KIM GORDON

ISBN: 978-0-9853567-0-5
1. JUVENILE FICTION/Christmas 2. JUVENILE
FICTION/Dragons & Mythical 3. JUVENILE
FICTION/Myths & Fables I. Title

Library of Congress Control Number: 2012918241

Printed in the United States of America
Bang Printing, Brainerd, Minnesota

First Printing: 2012

10 9 8 7 6 5 4 3 2 1

Romanian Dragons, LLC
1250 East Moore Lake Drive
Suite 240
Fridley, MN 55432
(612) 991-0564

To order, visit www.RomanianDragons.com

Acknowledgments

Susan, Laura and Gregory Ledray
Norma Rust
Kellie M. Hultgren, Editor
Writer's Guild, Priory of the Holy Grail
No Faults Tennis Team

This Book Belongs To:

_____

From:

_____

Someday you may see a dragon like me! I'm a tiny and usually invisible dragon. My kind is the swiftest of the unseen, and the most curious. I seek new places to learn by watching and listening. Then I return to Dragon Hollow in Romania, where I share my adventure and learn from others.

Before my return I experience dragon rest. Other creatures hibernate. I sleep unexpectedly in early winter. During dragon rest I cannot fly, and other creatures can see me. So I hide deep in a cave or hollow tree.

One year I saw two children playing games I'd never seen. I followed the boy and girl into their house and hid behind the top of a picture frame. I was sure I could get out through the door, but no one went outside. I was trapped, and dragon rest came upon me suddenly. I fell asleep.

I woke up and was surprised to see a dragon looking at me! It was my reflection in a window. Uh, oh. My shape and green eyes could be seen by anyone!

A pine tree had appeared inside the house, right next to my hiding place. It had been cut down and then made to stand up again. I did not understand. Why put a tree inside of a house?

Then I watched as the children and their parents put things upon it. Bright things. Small things. Even paper things. It soon looked very different from any tree I had ever seen.

Suddenly, the boy ran to the picture and yanked it from the wall. I tumbled through the air and landed in the tree. No one saw me. The girl hung up a new picture of a baby and some animals in the night, under a star. I felt suddenly tired, and I slept.

I awoke slowly, feeling uneasy. I could feel warm breath on my face. My eyes focused and stared into the girl's large brown eyes. Two blue eyes blinked nearby.

"Don't tell Mom and Dad," she whispered.

The boy frowned at her and asked, "How do you know it's alive?"

"I touched it. It feels alive," she replied softly. The boy stared at her in amazement. "I think it's afraid," she whispered.

I wanted to hide but fell asleep again.

I awoke staring into the stretched face of a green-eyed dragon. It was my reflection wrapped around a silver ball. I was in a different part of the tree, facing a new direction. They had moved me.

Suddenly, the tree shook. The silver ball disappeared, and the girl's eyes looked into mine. Then the boy's. I yawned, and as my teeth snapped back together I sparked! No gas came up from my belly, so there was no fire.

"It's a dragon for sure! Let's call it Sparky," the girl said. Then she picked me up and moved me again. They hung colored balls all around me. I saw a drop of water on the end of a tube coming from a bottle hidden in the branches. I touched my tongue to it and drank. Maybe they were afraid I would set the tree on fire. But I am a kind dragon. Soon I fell asleep again.

I awoke with a jolt. I was now facing the fireplace, where four large stockings hung from the mantel. The stockings were too large for anyone in the family to wear. They were a curiosity, this family!

I heard the children's father say, "There's a storm coming, but we'll be safe. It should warm up soon, and then we can go to town again. We have food, and the fire will keep us warm." Then it was quiet. After a while, the girl said, "Don't worry, Papa, we aren't afraid." The children's mother spoke, very softly, "Well, it's late, we must all go to bed now."

I must have slept again, because suddenly I awoke to a loud cracking sound. The house trembled as the old willow tree outside split and came crashing through the roof. Ice and snow covered the room, and the fire went out. Worried voices shouted all at once. Cold wind stabbed through the house as the parents began chopping and sawing on the fallen willow.

Then I heard the girl ask, "Can I help?"

"No, darling. Go back to bed and watch your brother. Stay under the covers and keep warm," her mother replied.

The girl turned and scurried back to bed.

They are worried, I thought. It is very cold. The house is broken, but now I can get out. But I fell asleep again.

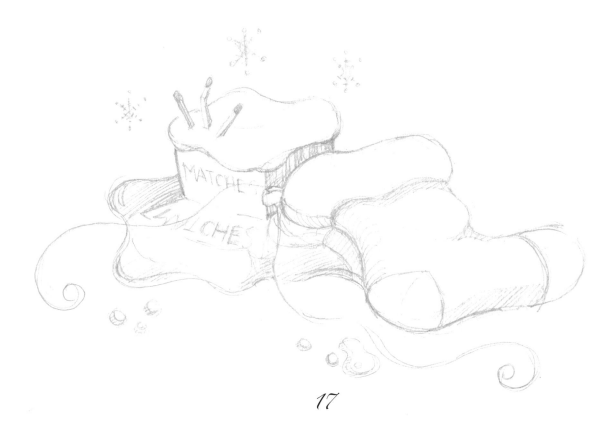

I awoke to a dreadful cold. The family was huddled together near the fireplace, wrapped in blankets. The father bent over tinder and small scraps of paper formed into a nest. His cold hands could not hold the match tightly. When he struck it against a rock, the match fell to the floor. The matchbox had fallen into the snow, and the matches were wet and ruined.

Arching my back, I stretched out my wings, knowing that my dragon's rest had ended. The girl turned and looked at my hiding place.

"There is a dragon in the Christmas tree that can help us," she said.

"It can make sparks in its mouth!" the boy said, excited. "We can put its head in the tinder and it will make sparks and start a fire."

They ran to the tree and looked behind the glass balls and the hanging things, their eyes darting from one branch to another.

I did not move. I was invisible. They all looked into the tree as the girl explained how she had found me and seen my sparks.

After a while the girl stopped looking.

"It's gone now," she said. The boy sighed deeply.

"You must believe us!" the boy cried.

"Well," his mother replied, "maybe it went back to its family."

The father closed his eyes for a second. Then he said, "It will be warmer tomorrow."

The woman took the man's cold hands in hers and rubbed them gently. She said, "It's Christmas, and we haven't opened a single present yet." The three looked at her, and she smiled through her worry. "Who will go first?"

"I will, Mama," the boy replied. He took a package from under the tree and opened it with excitement.

"Wow!" he said. It was something round that bounced up when it was thrown down.

The girl then opened her present very carefully. It was a package of clothes too small for anyone to wear. "For my doll!" she exclaimed. She ran out of the room and came back with a toy person. The small clothes fit perfectly, and her parents smiled.

"Thank you!" she said, and she handed her mother a package.

The woman untied the ribbon and pulled back the paper wrapping. It was an apron. She stood and put it on over her coat and danced as they all laughed, clouds of cold breath filling the air between them.

"Here's yours, Papa," the boy said as he handed his father a package. When he opened it, their eyes fell. It was a tin matchbox, but there were no matches inside.

"Well, this will keep our matches dry the next time something terrible happens," the father said. Then they all started singing. After listening for a bit, I decided they were singing about the baby in the picture.

I walked slowly to the end of my branch and sprang out. My left wing struck a glass ball as I launched into the air. It fell to the floor and rolled between the boy and the girl. They watched it but kept singing as I escaped through the hole in the roof.

I did not know exactly how we dragons find our way back to Romania. I just knew how high I must fly, and something would call me in the right direction. I felt very, very strong as I circled up into the starry sky. I heard the singing far below me, and I knew the family was numb with cold. Moonlight bounced off the tree's ornaments and lit the billowing fog of their singing.

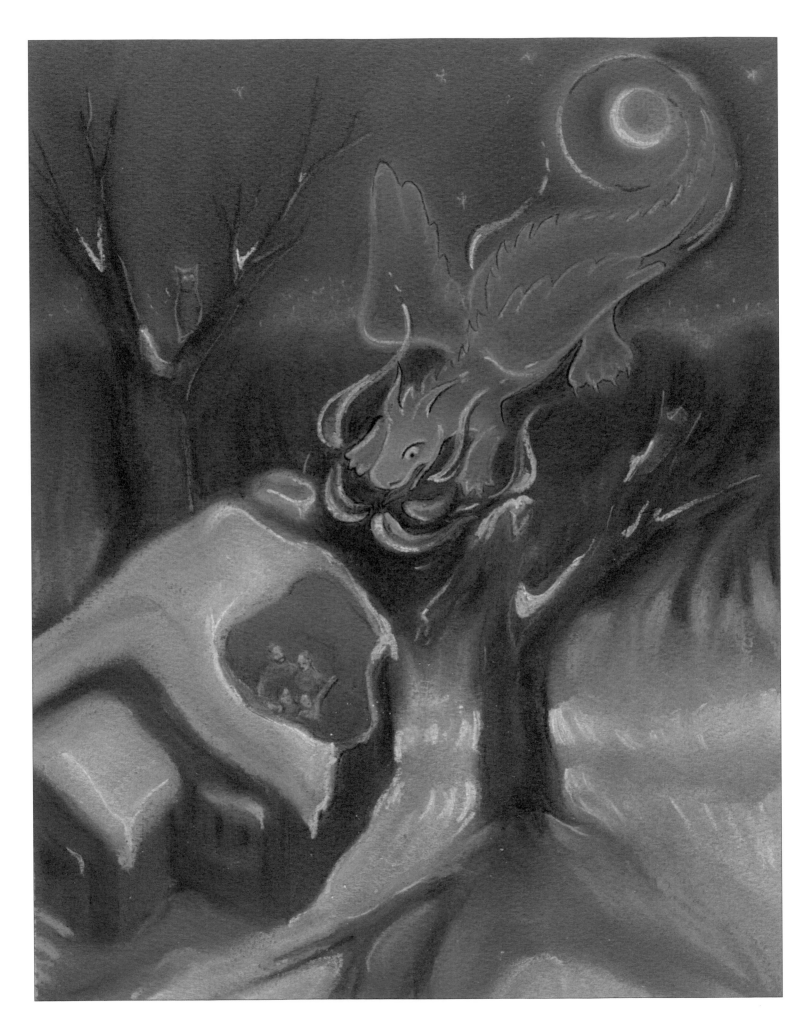

Like a falcon I streaked toward Earth from high above. A keen-eyed owl spun its head toward the sound of my wings, but it saw nothing in the moonlight. A mouse smelled something in the air and scurried away. I swooped through the hole in the roof and shot over the top of the strange indoor tree. Gas from my belly hissed between my teeth as I sparked. A streak of flame shot into the fireplace where the tinder nest lay. It burst into a ball of fire. The father jumped up and fed some dry branches to the hungry flame.

I flew into the tree, and my tail snapped against a silver bell. The family stared into the tree, toward the ringing. The fire's light danced across their astonished and grateful faces. I think each one of them knew that a tiny green-eyed dragon was watching them.

"Thank you, and merry Christmas, Sparky!" the girl whispered as I began my journey home.

The End